'He had the Ten Kings of Hell and their minions over in one small corner, and everything else – the entire screen – was enveloped in a fire-storm so terrible you thought the swirling flames were going to melt the Mountain of Sabres and the Forest of Swords'

RYŪNOSUKE AKUTAGAWA
Born 1 March 1892, Tokyo
Died 24 July 1927, Tokyo

'Hell Screen' and 'The Spider Thread' first published 1918.

ALSO PUBLISHED BY PENGUIN BOOKS

Rashōmon and Seventeen Other Stories

RYŪNOSUKE AKUTAGAWA

Hell Screen

TRANSLATED BY JAY RUBIN

PENGUIN BOOKS

PENGUIN CLASSICS

Published by the Penguin Group
Penguin Books Ltd, 80 Strand, London WC2R 0RL, England
Penguin Group (USA) Inc., 375 Hudson Street, New York, New York 10014, USA
Penguin Group (Canada), 90 Eglinton Avenue East, Suite 700, Toronto, Ontario,
Canada M4P 2Y3 (a division of Pearson Penguin Canada Inc.)
Penguin Ireland, 25 St Stephen's Green, Dublin 2, Ireland (a division of Penguin Books Ltd)
Penguin Group (Australia), 250 Camberwell Road, Camberwell, Victoria 3124, Australia
(a division of Pearson Australia Group Pty Ltd)
Penguin Books India Pvt Ltd, 11 Community Centre, Panchsheel Park,
New Delhi – 110 017, India
Penguin Group (NZ), 67 Apollo Drive, Rosedale, North Shore 0632, New Zealand
(a division of Pearson New Zealand Ltd)
Penguin Books (South Africa) (Pty) Ltd, 24 Sturdee Avenue, Rosebank, Johannesburg 2196,
South Africa

Penguin Books Ltd, Registered Offices: 80 Strand, London WC2R 0RL, England

www.penguin.com

Selected from *Rashōmon and Seventeen Other Stories* published by Penguin Books 2006
This edition published in Penguin Classics 2011
1

Translation copyright © Jay Rubin, 2006

Typeset by Jouve (UK), Milton Keynes
Printed in England by Clays Ltd, St Ives plc

ISBN: 978-0-141-19572-8

www.greenpenguin.co.uk

Penguin Books is committed to a sustainable future
for our business, our readers and our planet.
The book in your hands is made from paper
certified by the Forest Stewardship Council.

Contents

Hell Screen

I

I am certain there has never been anyone like our great Lord of Horikawa, and I doubt there ever will be another. In a dream before His Lordship was born, Her Maternal Ladyship saw the awesomely armed Guardian Deity of the West – or so people say. In any case, His Lordship seemed to have innate qualities that distinguished him from ordinary human beings. And because of this, his accomplishments never ceased to amaze us. You need only glance at his mansion in the Capital's Horikawa district to sense the boldness of its conception. Its – how shall I put it? – its grandeur, its heroic scale are beyond the reach of our mediocre minds. Some have questioned the wisdom of His Lordship's undertaking such a project, comparing him to China's First Emperor, whose subjects were forced to build the Great Wall, or to the Sui emperor Yang, who made his people erect lofty palaces; but such critics might be likened to the proverbial blind men who described the elephant according only to the parts they could feel. It was never His Lordship's intention to seek splendor and glory for himself alone. He was always a man of great magnanimity who shared his joys with the wider world, so to speak, and kept in mind even the lowliest of his subjects.

Surely this is why he was left unscathed by his encounter with that midnight procession of goblins so often seen at the lonely intersection of Nijō-Ōmiya in the Capital; it is also why, when rumor had it that the ghost of Tōru, Minister of the Left, was appearing night after night at the site of his ruined mansion by the river at Higashi-Sanjō (you must know it: where the minister had recreated the famous seascape of Shiogama in his garden), it took only a simple rebuke from His Lordship to make the spirit vanish. In the face of such resplendent majesty, no wonder all residents of the Capital – old and young, men and women – revered His Lordship as a reincarnation of the Buddha. One time, it is said, His Lordship was returning from a plum-blossom banquet at the Palace when the ox pulling his carriage got loose and injured an old man who happened to be passing by. The old fellow knelt and clasped his hands in prayerful thanks for having been caught on the horns of His Lordship's own ox!

So many, many stories about His Lordship have been handed down. His Imperial Majesty himself once presented His Lordship with thirty pure white horses on the occasion of a New Year's banquet. Another time, when construction of the Nagara Bridge seemed to be running counter to the will of the local deity, His Lordship offered up a favorite boy attendant as a human sacrifice to be buried at the foot of a pillar. And then there was the time when, to have a growth cut from his thigh, he summoned the Chinese monk who had brought the art of surgery to our country. Oh, there's no end to the tales! For sheer horror, though, none of them measures up to the story of the screen depicting scenes of hell which is now a prized family heirloom. Even His Lordship, normally so imperturbable, was horrified by what happened, and those of us who waited upon him – well, it goes without saying that we were shocked out of our minds. I myself had served as one of His Lordship's men for a full twenty years, but what I witnessed then was more terrible than anything I had ever – or *have* ever – experienced.

In order to tell you the story of the hell screen, however, I must first tell you about the painter who created it. His name was Yoshihide.

2

I suspect that even now there are ladies and gentlemen who would recognize the name 'Yoshihide.' He was famous back then as the greatest painter in the land, but he had reached the age of perhaps fifty, and he looked like nothing more than a thoroughly unpleasant little old man, all skin and bones. He dressed normally enough for his appearances at His Lordship's mansion – in a reddish-brown, broad-sleeved silk robe and a tall black hat with a soft bend to the right – but as a person he was anything but normal. You could see he had a mean streak, and his lips, unnaturally red for such an old man, gave a disturbing, bestial impression. Some people said the redness came from his moistening his paint brush with his lips, but I wonder about that. Crueler tongues used to say that he looked and moved like a monkey, and they went so far as to give Yoshihide the nickname 'Monkeyhide.'

Ah, that nickname reminds me of an episode. Yoshihide had a daughter, his only child – a sweet, lovely girl utterly unlike her father. She had been taken into the Horikawa mansion as a junior lady-in-waiting for His Lordship's own daughter, the Young Mistress. Perhaps because she lost her mother at a tender age, she had an unusually mature and deeply sympathetic nature and a cleverness beyond her years, and everyone from Her Ladyship on down loved the girl for her quickness to notice others' every need.

Around that time someone from the Tamba Province presented His Lordship with a tame monkey, and the Young Master, who was then at the height of his boyish naughtiness, decided to name it 'Yoshihide.' The monkey was a funny-looking little creature as it was, but capping it with that name gave everyone in the household a hearty laugh. Oh, if only they had been satisfied just to laugh! But whatever the monkey did – whether climbing to the top of the garden pine, or soiling the mats of a staff member's room – people would find a reason to torment it, and always with a shout of 'Yoshihide!'

Then one day, as Yoshihide's daughter was gliding down a long outdoor corridor to deliver a note gaily knotted on a branch of red winter plum, the monkey Yoshihide darted in through the sliding door at the far end, in full flight from something. The animal was running with a limp and seemed unable to climb a post as it often did when frightened. Then who should appear chasing after it but the Young Master, brandishing a switch and shouting, 'Come back here, you tangerine thief! Come back here!' Yoshihide's daughter drew up short at the sight, and the monkey clung to her skirts with a pitiful cry. This must have aroused her compassion, for, still holding the plum branch in one hand, she swept the monkey up in the soft folds of her lavender sleeve. Then, giving a little bow to the Young Master, she said with cool clarity, 'Forgive me for interfering, my young lord, but he is just an animal. Please pardon him.'

Temper still up from the chase, the Young Master scowled and stamped his foot several times. 'Why are you protecting him?' he demanded. 'He stole my tangerine!'

'He is just an animal,' she repeated. 'He doesn't know any better.' And then, smiling sadly, she added, 'His name is Yoshihide, after all. I can't just stand by and watch "my father" being punished.' This was apparently enough to break the Young Master's will.

'All right, then,' he said with obvious reluctance. 'If you're pleading for your father's life, I'll let him off this time.'

The Young Master flung his switch into the garden and stalked back out through the sliding door.

3

After this incident, Yoshihide's daughter and the little monkey grew close. The girl had a golden bell that her young mistress had given her, which she hung from the monkey's neck on a pretty crimson cord. And he, for his part, would almost never leave her side. Once, when she was in bed with a cold, the monkey spent hours by her pillow, biting its nails, and I swear it had a worried look on its face.

Then, strangely enough, people stopped teasing the monkey. In fact, they began treating it with special kindness, until even the Young Master would occasionally throw it a persimmon or a chestnut, and I heard he once flew into a rage when one of the samurai kicked the animal. Soon after that, His Lordship himself ordered the girl to appear before him with the monkey in her arms – all because, in hearing about the Young Master's tantrum, I am told, he naturally also heard about how the girl had come to care for the monkey.

'I admire your filial behavior,' His Lordship said. 'Here, take this.' And he presented her with a fine scarlet underrobe. They tell me that his Lordship was especially pleased when the monkey, imitating the girl's expression of gratitude, bowed low before him, holding the robe aloft. And so His Lordship's partiality for the girl was born entirely from his wish to commend her filial devotion to her father and not, as rumor had it, from any physical attraction he might have felt for her. Not that such suspicions were entirely groundless, but there will be time for me to tell you about that later. For now, suffice it to say that His Lordship was not the sort of person to lavish his affections on the daughter of a mere painter, however beautiful she might be.

Well, then, having been singled out for praise this way, Yoshihide's daughter withdrew from His Lordship's presence, but she knew how to avoid provoking the envy of the household's other, less modest, ladies-in-waiting. Indeed, people grew fonder than ever of her and the monkey, and the Young Mistress almost never let them leave her side, even bringing them with her in her ox-drawn carriage when she went to observe shrine rituals and the like.

But enough about the girl for now. Let me continue with my story of her father, Yoshihide. As I have said, the monkey Yoshihide quickly became everyone's little darling, but Yoshihide himself remained an object of universal scorn, reviled as 'Monkeyhide' by everyone behind his back. And not only in the Horikawa mansion. Even such an eminent Buddhist prelate as the Abbot of Yokawa hated Yoshihide so much that the very mention of his name was enough to make him turn purple as if he had seen a devil. (Some said this was because Yoshihide had drawn a caricature ridiculing certain aspects of the Abbot's behavior, but this was merely a rumor that circulated among the lower classes and as such can hardly be credited.) In any case, Yoshi-hide's reputation was so bad that anyone you asked would have told you the same thing. If there were those who spoke kindly of Yoshihide, they were either a handful of the brotherhood of painters or else people who knew his work but not the man himself.

His appearance was not the only thing that people hated about Yoshihide. In fact, he had many evil traits that repelled them even more, and for which he had only himself to blame.

4

For one thing, Yoshihide was a terrible miser; he was harsh in his dealings with people; he had no shame; he was lazy and greedy. But worst of all, he was insolent and arrogant. He never let you forget that he was 'the greatest painter in the land.' Nor was his arrogance limited to painting. He could not be satisfied till he displayed his contempt for every custom and convention that ordinary people practiced. A man who was his apprentice for many years once told me this story: Yoshihide was present one day in the mansion of a certain gentleman when the celebrated Shamaness of the Cypress Enclosure was there, undergoing spirit possession. The woman delivered a horrifying message from the spirit, but Yoshihide was unimpressed. He took up a handy ink brush and did a detailed sketch of her wild expression as if he viewed spirit possession as mere trickery.

No wonder, then, that such a man would commit acts of sacrilege in his work: in painting the lovely goddess Kisshōten, he used the face of a common harlot, and to portray the mighty flame-draped Fudō, his model was a criminal released to do chores in the Magistrate's office. If you tried to warn him that he was flirting with danger, he would respond with feigned innocence. '*I'm* the one who painted them, after all,' he would say. 'Are you trying to tell me that my own Buddhas and gods are going to punish me?' Even his apprentices were shocked by this. I myself knew several of them who, fearing for their own punishment in the afterlife, wasted no time in leaving his employ. The man's arrogance simply knew no bounds. He was convinced that he was the greatest human being under heaven.

It goes without saying that Yoshihide lorded it over the other painters of his time. True, his brushwork and colors were utterly different from theirs, and so the many painters with whom he was on bad terms tended to speak of him as a charlatan. They rhapsodized over the work of old masters such as Kawanari or Kanaoka ('On moonlit nights you could actually *smell* the plum blossoms painted on that wooden door,' or 'You could actually *hear* the courtier on that screen playing his flute'), but all they had to say about Yoshihide's work was how eerie and unsettling they found it. Take his *Five Levels of Rebirth* on the Ryūgaiji temple gate, for example. 'When I passed the gate late at night,' one said, 'I could hear the dying celestials sighing and sobbing.' 'That's nothing,' another claimed. 'I could smell the flesh of the dead rotting.' 'And how about the portraits of the household's ladies-in-waiting that His Lordship ordered from Yoshihide? Every single woman he painted fell ill and died within three years. It was as if he had snatched their very souls from them.' According to one of his harshest critics, this was the final proof that Yoshihide practiced the Devil's Art.

But Yoshihide was so perverse, as I've said, that remarks like this only filled him with pride. When His Lordship joked to him one time, 'For you, it seems, the uglier the better,' old Yoshihide's far-too-red lips spread in an eerie grin and he replied imperiously, 'Yes, My Lord, it's true. Other painters are such mediocrities, they cannot appreciate the beauty of ugliness.' I must say, 'Greatest Painter in the Land' or not, it was incredible that he could spout such self-congratulatory nonsense in His Lordship's presence! No wonder his apprentices called him Chira Eiju behind his back! You know: Chira Eiju, the long-nosed goblin who crossed over from China long ago to spread the sin of arrogance.

But still, even Yoshihide, in all his incredible perversity – yes, even Yoshihide displayed human tenderness when it came to one thing.

5

By this I mean that Yoshihide was truly mad about his only daughter, the young lady-in-waiting. The girl was, as I said before, a wonderfully kind-hearted young creature deeply devoted to her father, and his love for her was no less strong than hers for him. I gather that he provided for her every need – every robe, every hair ornament – without the slightest objection. Don't you find this incredible for a man who had never made a single contribution to a temple?

Yoshihide's love for his daughter, however, remained just that: love. It never occurred to him that he should be trying to find her a good husband someday. Far from it: he was not above hiring street thugs to beat up anyone who might make improper advances to her. So even when His Lordship honored her with the position of junior lady-in-waiting in his own household, Yoshihide was far from happy about it, and for a while he always wore a sour expression whenever he was in His Lordship's presence. I have no doubt that people who witnessed this display were the ones who began speculating that His Lordship had been attracted to the girl's beauty when he ordered her into service despite her father's objections.

Such rumors were entirely false, of course. It was nothing but Yoshihide's obsessive love for his daughter that kept him wishing to have her step down from service, that is certain. I remember the time His Lordship ordered Yoshihide to do a painting of Monju as a child, and Yoshihide pleased him greatly with a marvelous work that used one of His Lordship's own boy favorites as a model. 'You can have anything you want as your reward,' said His Lordship. 'Anything at all.'

Yoshihide should have been awestruck to hear such praise from His Lordship's own lips, and he did in fact prostrate himself in thanks before him, but can you imagine what he asked? 'If it please Your Lordship, I beg you to return my daughter to her former lowly state.' The impudence of the man! This was no ordinary household, after all. No matter how much he loved his daughter, to beg for her release from service in privileged proximity to the great Lord of Horikawa himself – where in the world does one find such audacity? Not even a man as grandly magnanimous as His Lordship could help feeling some small annoyance at such a request, as was evident from the way he stared at Yoshihide for a while in silence.

Presently he spoke: 'That will not happen,' he said, all but spitting out the words, and he abruptly withdrew.

This was not the first nor the last such incident: I think there might have been four or five in all. And with each repetition, it seemed to me, His Lordship gazed on Yoshihide with increasing coldness. The girl, for her part, seemed to fear for her father's welfare. Often she could be seen sobbing quietly to herself in her room, teeth clamped on her sleeve. All this only reinforced the rumor that His Lordship was enamored of the girl. People also said that the command to paint the screen had something to do with her rejection of His Lordship's advances, but that, of course, could not be so.

As I see it, it was entirely out of pity for the girl's situation that His Lordship refused to let her go. I am certain he believed, with great generosity, that she would be far better off if he were to keep her in his mansion and enable her to live in comfort than if he sent her back to her hardheaded old father. That he was partial to her, of course, there could be no doubt: she was such a sweet-tempered young thing. But to assert that he took his lustful pleasure with her is a view that springs from twisted reasoning. No, I would have to call it a groundless falsehood.

At any rate, owing to these matters regarding his daughter, this was a period when Yoshihide was in great disfavor with His Lordship. Suddenly one day, for whatever reason, His Lordship summoned Yoshihide and ordered him to paint a folding screen portraying scenes from the eight Buddhist hells.

6

Oh, that screen! I can almost see its terrifying images of hell before me now!

Other artists painted what they called images of hell, but their compositions were nothing like Yoshihide's. He had the Ten Kings of Hell and their minions over in one small corner, and everything else – the entire screen – was enveloped in a firestorm so terrible you thought the swirling flames were going to melt the Mountain of Sabers and the Forest of Swords. Aside from the vaguely Chinese costumes of the Judges of the Dark, with their swatches of yellow and indigo, all you saw was the searing color of flames and, dancing wildly among them, black smoke clouds of hurled India ink and flying sparks of blown-on gold dust.

These alone were enough to shock and amaze any viewer, but the sinners writhing in the hellfire of Yoshi-hide's powerful brush had nothing in common with those to be seen in ordinary pictures of hell. For Yoshi-hide had included sinners from all stations in life, from the most brilliant luminary of His Majesty's exalted circle to the basest beggar and outcast. A courtier in magnificent ceremonial vestments, a nubile lady-in-waiting in five-layered robes, a rosary-clutching priest intoning the holy name of Amida, a samurai student on high wooden clogs, an aristocratic little girl in a simple shift, a Yin-Yang diviner swishing his paper wand through the air: I could never name them all. But there they were, human beings of every kind, inundated by smoke and flame, tormented by wardens of hell with their heads of bulls and horses, and driven in all directions like autumn leaves scattering before a great wind. 'Oh, look at that one,' you would say, 'the one with her hair all tangled up in a forked lance and her arms and legs drawn in tighter than a spider's: could she be one of those shrine maidens who perform for the gods? And, oh, *that* fellow there, hanging upside-down like a bat, his breast pierced by a short lance: surely he is supposed to be a greenhorn provincial governor.' And the kinds of torture were as numberless as the sinners themselves – flogging with an iron scourge, crushing under a gigantic rock, pecking by a monstrous bird, grinding in the jaws of a poisonous serpent . . .

But surely the single most horrifying image of all was that of a carriage plummeting through space. As it fell, it grazed the upper boughs of a sword tree, where clumps of corpses were skewered on fang-like branches. Blasts of hell wind swept up the carriage curtains to reveal a court lady so gorgeously appareled she might have been one of His Imperial Majesty's own Consorts or Intimates, her straight black hip-length hair flying upward in the flames, the full whiteness of her throat laid bare as she writhed in agony. Every detail of the woman's form and the blazing carriage filled the viewer with an agonizing sense of the hideous torments to be found in the Hell of Searing Heat. The sheer horror of the entire screen – might I say? – seemed to be concentrated in this one figure. It had been executed with such inspired workmanship, you'd think that all who saw it could hear the woman's dreadful screams.

Oh yes, this was it: for the sake of painting this one image, the terrible event occurred. Otherwise, how could even the great Yoshihide have painted hell's torments so vividly? It was his cruel fate to lose his life in exchange for completing the screen. In a sense, the hell in his painting was the hell into which Yoshihide himself, the greatest painter in the realm, was doomed one day to fall.

I am afraid that, in my haste to speak of the screen with its unusual images of hell, I may have reversed the order of my story. Now let me continue with the part about Yoshihide when he received His Lordship's command to do a painting of hell.

7

For nearly six months after the commission, Yoshihide poured all his energy into the screen, never once calling at His Lordship's residence. Don't you find it strange that such a doting father should abandon all thought of seeing his daughter once he had started on a painting? According to the apprentice I mentioned earlier, Yoshihide always approached his work like a man possessed by a fox spirit. In fact, people used to say that the only reason Yoshihide was able to make such a name for himself in art was that he had pledged his soul to one of the great gods of fortune; what proved it was that if you peeked in on him when he was painting, you could always see shadowy fox spirits swarming all around him. What this means, I suspect, is that, once he picked up his brush, Yoshihide thought of nothing else but completing the painting before him. He would spend all day and night shut up in his studio out of sight. His concentration seems to have been especially intense when he was working on this particular screen with its images of hell.

This is not merely to say that he would keep the latticed shutters pulled down and spend all day by the tripod oil lamp, mixing secret combinations of paint or posing his apprentices in various costumes for him to sketch. No, that was normal behavior for the working Yoshihide, even before this screen. Remember, this was the man who, when he was painting his *Five Levels of Rebirth* on the Ryūgaiji temple gate, went out specially to inspect a corpse lying on the roadside – the kind of sight from which any ordinary person would recoil – and spent hours sitting before it, sketching its rotting face and limbs without missing a hair. I don't blame you, then, if you are among those who cannot imagine what I mean when I say that his concentration during his work on the hell screen was especially intense. I haven't time now to explain this in detail, but I can at least tell you the most important things.

One day an apprentice of Yoshihide's (the one I've mentioned a few times already) was busy dissolving pigments when the master suddenly said to him, 'I'm planning to take a nap but, I don't know, I've been having bad dreams lately.'

There was nothing strange about this, so the apprentice merely answered, 'I see, Sir,' and continued with his work.

Yoshihide, however, was not his usual self. Somewhat hesitantly, and with a doleful look on his face, he made a surprising request: 'I want you to sit and work beside me while I sleep.'

The apprentice thought it rather odd that his master should be worrying about dreams, but it was a simple enough request and he promptly agreed to it.

'All right, then,' Yoshihide said, still looking worried, 'come inside right away.' He hesitated. 'And when the other apprentices arrive,' he added, 'don't let any of them in where I am sleeping.'

'Inside' meant the room where the master actually did his painting, and as usual on this day, the apprentice told me, its doors and windows were shut as tightly as at night. In the dull glow of an oil lamp stood the large folding screen, its panels arranged in a semi-circle and still only sketched out in charcoal. Yoshihide lay down with his head pillowed on his forearm and slipped into the deep sleep of an utterly exhausted man. Hardly any time had gone by, however, when the apprentice began to hear a sound that he had no way of describing. It was a voice, he told me, but a strange and eerie one.

8

At first, it was just a sound, but soon, in snatches, the voice began to form words that came to him as if from under water, like the muffled cries of a drowning man. 'Wha-a-a-t?' the voice said. 'You want me to come with you? . . . Where? Where are you taking me? To hell, you say. To the Hell of Searing Heat, you say. Who . . . who are you, damn you? Who can you be but –'

The apprentice, dissolving pigments, felt his hands stop of their own accord. He peered fearfully through the gloom at his master's face. Not only had the furrowed skin gone stark white, but fat beads of sweat oozed from it, and the dry-lipped, snaggle-toothed mouth strained wide open as if gasping for breath. The youth saw something moving in his master's mouth with dizzying speed, like an object being yanked by a cord, but then – imagine! – he realized the thing was Yoshihide's tongue. The fragmented speech had been coming from that tongue of his.

'Who could it be but – *you*, damn you. It *is* you! I thought so! What's that? You've come to show me the way there? You want me to follow you. To hell! My daughter is waiting for me in hell!'

The apprentice told me that an uncanny feeling overcame him at that point – his eyes seemed to make out vague, misshapen shadows that slid over the surface of the screen and flooded down upon the two of them. Naturally, he immediately reached over and shook Yoshihide as hard as he could; but rather than waking, the master, in a dreamlike state, went on talking to himself and showed no sign of regaining consciousness. Desperate now, the apprentice grabbed the jar for washing brushes and splashed all the water into Yoshihide's face.

'I'm waiting for you,' Yoshihide was saying, 'so hurry and get into the cart. Come along to hell!' But the moment the water hit him his words turned to a strangled moan. At last he opened his eyes, and he sprang up more wildly than if he had been jabbed with a needle. But the misshapen creatures must have been with him still, for he stared into space, with mouth agape and with terrified eyes. At length he returned to himself and, without a hint of gratitude, barked at the poor apprentice, 'I'm all right now. Get out of here.'

The apprentice knew he would be scolded if he resisted his master at a time like this, so he hurried out of the room, but he told me that when he saw the sunlight again he felt as relieved as if he were waking from his own nightmare.

This was by no means Yoshihide at his worst, however. A month later he called yet another apprentice into the inner room. The young man found Yoshihide standing in the gloom of the oil lamps biting the end of his paintbrush. Without a moment's hesitation, Yoshihide turned to him and said, 'Sorry, but I need you naked again.' The master had ordered such things in the past, so the apprentice quickly stripped off his clothes, but now Yoshihide said with a strange scowl, 'I want to see a person in chains, so do what I tell you. Sorry about this, but it will just take a little while.' Yoshihide could mouth apologetic phrases, but he issued his cold commands without the least show of sympathy. This particular apprentice was a well-built lad who looked more suited to wielding a sword than a paintbrush, but even he must have been shocked by what happened. 'I figured the Master had gone crazy and was going to kill me,' he told people again and again long afterward. Yoshihide was apparently annoyed by the young man's slow preparations. Instead of waiting, he dragged out a narrow iron chain from heaven knows where and all but pounced on the apprentice's back, wrenching the man's arms behind him and winding him in the chain. Then he gave the end of the chain a cruel yank and sent the young man crashing down on the floor.

9

The apprentice lay there like – what? – like a keg of saké that someone had knocked over. Legs and arms mercilessly contorted, he could move only his head. And with the chain cutting off the circulation of his blood, you know, his skin swelled red – face, torso, everywhere. Yoshihide, though, was apparently not the least bit concerned to see him like this; he circled this saké-keg of a body, observing it from every angle and drawing sketch after sketch. I am certain that, without my spelling it out, you can imagine what torture this must have been for the poor apprentice.

If nothing had interrupted it, the young man's ordeal would almost surely have lasted even longer, but fortunately (or perhaps unfortunately) a narrow, winding streak like black oil began to flow from behind a large jar in the corner of the room. At first it moved slowly, like a thick liquid, but then it began to slide along the floor more smoothly, glinting in the darkness until it was almost touching the apprentice's nose. He took a good look at it, gasped and screamed, 'A snake! A snake!' The way he described the moment to me, he felt as if every drop of blood in his body would freeze, which I can well understand, for in fact the snake's cold tongue was just about to touch the flesh of his neck where the chain was biting. Even Yoshihide, for all his perversity, must have felt a rush of horror at this unforeseeable occurrence. Flinging his brush down, he bent and gripped the snake by the tail, dangling it upside-down. The snake raised its head and began to coil upward around its own body, but it could not reach Yoshihide's hand.

'You cost me a good brush stroke, damn you,' he growled at the snake, flinging it into the jar in the corner. Then, with obvious reluctance, he loosened the chains that bound the apprentice's body. In fact, loosening the chains was as far as he was willing to go: for the youth himself he spared not a word of sympathy. I suspect he was more enraged at having botched a single brush stroke than concerned that his apprentice might have been bitten by a snake. I heard afterward that he had been keeping the snake to sketch from.

I imagine that what little you have heard is enough for you to grasp the fanatic intensity with which Yoshihide approached his work. But let me give you one last terrible example concerning a young apprentice – no more than thirteen or fourteen – who could have lost his life for the hell screen. It happened one night when the boy, whose skin was fair as a girl's, was called into the master's studio. There he found Yoshihide by the tripod lamp balancing a piece of raw meat on his palm and feeding it to a bird the likes of which he had never seen before. The bird was the size of a cat, and in fact, with its two feather tufts sticking out from its head like ears and its big, round amber-colored eyes, it did look very much like a cat.

10

Yoshihide was a man who simply hated to have anyone pry into his business, and – the snake I told you about was one such case – he would never let his apprentices know what kinds of things he had in his studio. Depending on the subject he happened to be painting at the time, he might have a human skull perched on his table, or rows of silver bowls and gold-lacquered stands – you never knew. And his helpers told me they had no idea where he kept such things when he was not using them. This was surely one reason for the rumor that Yoshihide was the beneficiary of miraculous aid from a god of fortune.

Well then, the young apprentice, assuming for himself that the strange bird on the table was a model Yoshihide needed for the hell screen, knelt before the painter and asked in all humility, 'How can I help you, Master?'

Almost as if he had not heard the boy speak, Yoshi-hide licked his red lips and jerked his chin toward the bird. 'Not bad, eh? Look how tame it is.'

'Please tell me, Master, what is it? I have never seen anything like it before,' the boy said, keeping his wary gaze fixed on the cat-like bird with ears.

'What? Never seen anything like it?' Yoshihide respond-ed with his familiar scornful laugh. 'That's what you get for growing up in the Capital! It's a bird. A horned owl. A hunter brought it to me a few days ago from Mount Kurama. Only, you don't usually find them so tame.'

As he spoke, Yoshihide slowly raised his hand and gave a soft upward stroke to the feathers of the owl's back just as the bird finished swallowing the chunk of meat. Instantly the bird emitted a shriek and leaped from the table top, aiming its outstretched talons at the apprentice's face. Had the boy not shot his arm out to protect himself, I have no doubt that he would have ended up with more than a gash or two on his face. He cried out and shook his sleeve in an attempt to sweep the bird away, which only added to the fury of the attack. Beak clattering, the owl lunged at him again. Disre-garding Yoshihide's presence, the apprentice ran wildly around the cramped room, now standing to defend

27

himself, now crouching to drive the bird away. The monster, of course, stuck with him, flying up when he stood up and down when he crouched down, and using any opening to go straight for his eyes. With each lunge came a tremendous flapping of wings that filled the boy with dread. He felt so lost, he said later, that the familiar studio felt like a haunted valley deep in the mountains, with the smell of rotting leaves, the spray of a waterfall, the sour fumes of fruit stashed away by a monkey; even the dim glow of the master's oil lamp on its tripod looked to him like misty moonlight in the hills.

Being attacked by the owl, however, was not what most frightened the lad. What really made his flesh crawl was the way the master Yoshihide followed the commotion with his cold stare, taking his time to spread out a piece of paper, lick his brush, and then set about capturing the terrible image of a delicate boy being tormented by a hideous bird. At the sight, the apprentice was overcome by an inexpressible terror. For a time, he says, he even thought his master might kill him.

11

And you actually couldn't say that such a thing was out of the question. For it did seem that Yoshihide's sole purpose in calling the apprentice to his studio that night had been to set the owl on him and draw him trying to escape. Thus, when the apprentice caught that glimpse of his master at work, he felt his arms come up to protect his head and heard an incoherent scream escape his throat as he slumped down against the sliding door in the corner of the room. In that same instant Yoshihide himself cried out and jumped to his feet, whereupon the beating of the owl's wings grew faster and louder and there came the clatter of something falling over and a tearing sound. Having covered his head in terror, the apprentice now raised it again to find that the room had gone pitch dark, and he heard Yoshihide's angry voice calling to the other apprentices.

Eventually there was a far-off cry in response, and soon an apprentice rushed in with a lantern held high. In its sooty-smelling glow, the boy saw the tripod collapsed on the floor and the mats and planking soaked in the oil of the overturned lamp. He saw the owl, too, beating one wing in apparent pain as it flopped around the room. On the far side of the table, looking stunned, Yoshihide was raising himself from the floor and muttering something incomprehensible. And no wonder! That black snake was tightly coiled around the owl from neck to tail and over one wing. The apprentice had probably knocked the jar over as he slumped to the floor, and when the snake crawled out, the owl must have made the mistake of trying to grab it in its talons, only to give rise to this struggle. The two apprentices gaped at the bizarre scene and at each other until, with a silent bow to the master, they slipped out of the room. What happened to the owl and snake after that, no one knows.

This was by no means the only such incident. I forgot to mention that it was the beginning of autumn when His Lordship commanded Yoshihide to paint the hell screen; from then until the end of winter the apprentices were continually subjected to their master's frightening behavior. At that point, however, something seemed to interfere with Yoshihide's work on the screen. An even deeper layer of gloom came to settle over him, and he spoke to his assistants in markedly harsher tones. The screen was perhaps eight-tenths finished, but it showed no further signs of progress. Indeed, Yoshihide occasionally seemed to be on the verge of painting over those parts that he had already completed.

No one knew what he was finding so difficult about the screen, and what's more, no one tried to find out. Stung by those earlier incidents, his apprentices felt as if they were locked in a cage with a tiger or a wolf, and they found ways to keep their distance from the master.

12

For that reason, I have little to tell you about that period. The only unusual thing I can think of is that the hard-headed old codger suddenly turned weepy; people would often see him shedding tears when he was alone. An apprentice told me that one day he walked into the garden and saw the master standing on the veranda, gazing blankly at the sky with its promise of spring, his eyes full of tears. Embarrassed for the old man, the apprentice says, he silently withdrew. Don't you find it odd that this arrogant man, who went so far as to sketch a corpse on the roadside for his *Five Levels of Rebirth*, would cry like an infant just because the painting of the screen wasn't going as well as he wanted it to?

In any case, while Yoshihide was madly absorbed in his work on the screen, his daughter began to show increasing signs of melancholy, until the rest of us could see that she was often fighting back her tears. A pale, reserved, sad-faced girl to begin with, she took on a genuinely mournful aspect as her lashes grew heavy and shadows began to form around her eyes. This gave rise to all sorts of speculation – that she was worried about her father, or that she was suffering the pangs of love – but soon people were saying that it was all because

His Lordship was trying to bend her to his will. Then the gossiping ground to a halt, as though everyone had suddenly forgotten about her.

A certain event occurred at that time. Well after the first watch of the night, I was walking down an outdoor corridor when the monkey Yoshihide came flying at me from out of nowhere and started tugging at my trouser skirts. As I recall it, this was one of those warm early spring nights when you expect at any time now to be catching the romantic fragrance of plum blossoms in the pale moonlight. But what did I see in the moon's faint glow? It was the monkey baring its white fangs, wrinkling up its nose, and shrieking with almost manic intensity. An eerie chill was only three parts of what I felt: the other seven parts were anger at having my new trousers yanked at like that, and I considered kicking the beast aside and continuing on my way. I quickly changed my mind, however, recalling the case of the samurai who had earned the Young Master's displeasure by tormenting the monkey. And besides, the way the monkey was behaving, there was obviously something wrong. I therefore gave up trying to resist and allowed myself to be pulled several paces farther.

Where the corridor turned a corner, the pale surface of His Lordship's pond could be seen stretching off through the darkness beyond a gently drooping pine.

When the animal led me to that point, my ears were assaulted by the frantic yet strangely muffled sounds of what I took to be a struggle in a nearby room. All else was hushed. I heard no voices, no sounds but the splash of a fish leaping in the mingled moonlight and fog. The sound of the struggle brought me up short. If this was an intruder, I resolved, I would teach him a lesson, and, holding my breath, I edged closer to the sliding door.

13

My approach, however, was obviously too slow and cautious for the monkey. Yoshihide scampered around me in circles – once, twice, three times – then bounded up to my shoulder with a strangled cry. Instinctively, I jerked my head aside to avoid being scratched. The monkey dug its claws into my sleeve to keep from slipping down. This sent me staggering, and I stumbled backward, slamming against the door. Now I could no longer hesitate. I shot the door open and crouched to spring in beyond the moonlight's edge. At that very moment something rose up to block my view. With a start I realized it was a woman. She flew toward me as if someone had flung her out of the room. She nearly hit me but instead she tumbled forward and – why, I could not tell – went down on one knee before me, trembling and breathless, and staring up at me as if at some terrifying sight.

I am sure I need not tell you it was Yoshihide's daughter. That night, however, my eyes beheld her with a new vividness, as though she were an utterly different person. Her eyes were huge and shining. And her cheeks seemed to be burning red. Her disheveled clothes gave her an erotic allure that contrasted sharply with her usual childish innocence. Could this actually be the daughter of Yoshihide? I wondered – that frail-looking girl so modest and self-effacing in all things? Leaning against the sliding wooden door, I stared at this beautiful girl in the moonlight and then, as if they were capable of pointing, I flicked my eyes toward the hurried footsteps receding into the distance to ask her soundlessly, *Who was that?*

The girl bit her lip and shook her head in silence. I could see she felt deeply mortified.

I bent over her and, speaking softly next to her ear, now put my question into words: 'Who was that?' But again she refused to answer and would only shake her head. Indeed, she bit her lip harder than ever as tears gathered on her long lashes.

Born stupid, I can never understand anything that isn't perfectly obvious, and so I had no idea what to say to her. I could do nothing but stand there, feeling as if my only purpose was to listen to the wild beating of her heart. Of course, one thing that kept me silent was the conviction that it would be wrong of me to question her any further.

How long this went on, I do not know, but eventually I slid shut the door and gently told the girl, 'Go to your room now.' Her agitation seemed to have subsided somewhat. Assailed by an uneasy feeling that I had seen something I was not meant to see, and a sense of shame toward anyone and no one in particular, I began to pad my way back up the corridor. I had hardly walked ten paces, however, when again I felt a tug – a timid one – at the skirt of my trousers. I whirled around, startled, but what do you think it was?

I looked down to find the monkey Yoshihide prostrating himself at my feet, hands on the floor like a human being, bowing over and over in thanks, his golden bell ringing.

14

Perhaps two weeks went by after that. All of a sudden, Yoshihide arrived at the mansion to beg a personal audience with His Lordship. He probably dared do such a thing despite his humble station because he had long been in His Lordship's special favor. His Lordship rarely allowed anyone to come into his presence, but that day, as so often before, he assented readily to Yoshihide's request and had him shown in without a moment's delay. The man wore his usual reddish-brown robe and tall black soft hat. His face revealed a new level of sullenness, but he went down on all fours before His Lordship and at length, eyes down, he began to speak in husky tones:

'I come into your honored presence this day, My Lord, regarding the screen bearing images of hell which His Lordship ordered me to paint. I have applied myself to it day and night – outdone myself – such that my efforts have begun to bear fruit, and it is largely finished.'

'This is excellent news. I am very pleased.'

Even as His Lordship spoke these words, however, his voice seemed oddly lacking in power and vitality.

'No, My Lord, I am afraid the news is anything but excellent,' said Yoshihide, his eyes still fastened on the floor in a way that hinted at anger. 'The work may be largely finished, but there is still a part that I am unable to paint.'

'What? Unable to paint?'

'Indeed, sir. As a rule, I can only paint what I have seen. Or even if I succeed in painting something unknown to me, I myself cannot be satisfied with it. This is the same as not being able to paint it, does His Lordship not agree?'

As His Lordship listened to Yoshihide's words, his face gradually took on a mocking smile.

'Which would mean that if you wanted to paint a screen depicting hell, you would have to have seen hell itself.'

'Exactly, My Lord. In the great fire some years ago, though, I saw flames with my own eyes that I could use for those of the Hell of Searing Heat. In fact, I succeeded with my *Fudō of Twisting Flames* only because I experienced that fire. I believe My Lord is familiar with the painting.'

'What about sinners, though? And hell wardens – you have never seen those, have you?' His Lordship challenged Yoshihide with one question after another as though he had not heard Yoshihide's words.

'I have seen a person bound in iron chains,' said Yoshihide. 'And I have done a detailed sketch of someone being tormented by a monstrous bird. No, I think it cannot be said that I have never seen sinners being tortured. And as for hell wardens,' said Yoshihide, breaking into an eerie smile, 'my eyes have beheld them any number of times as I drift between sleeping and waking. The bull-headed ones, the horse-headed ones, the three-faced, six-armed devils: almost every night they come to torture me with their soundless clapping hands, their voiceless gaping mouths. No, they are not the ones I am having so much difficulty painting.'

I suspect this shocked even His Lordship. For a long while he only glared at Yoshihide until, with an angry twitch of the brow, he spat out, 'All right, then. What is it that you say you are unable to paint?'

15

'In the center of the screen, falling from the sky, I want to paint an aristocrat's carriage, its cabin woven of the finest split palm leaf.' As he spoke, Yoshihide raised himself to look directly at His Lordship for the first time – and with a penetrating gaze. I had heard that Yoshihide could be like a madman where painting was concerned; to me the look in his eyes at that moment was terrifying in that very way.

'In the carriage, a voluptuous noblewoman writhes in agony, her long black hair tossing in the ferocious flames. Her face . . . well, perhaps she contorts her brows and casts her gaze skyward toward the ceiling of the cabin as she chokes on the rising clouds of smoke. Her hands might tear at the cloth streamers of the carriage blinds as she struggles to ward off the shower of sparks raining down upon her. Around her swarm fierce, carnivorous birds, perhaps a dozen or more, snapping their beaks in anticipation – oh, My Lord, it is this, this image of the noblewoman in the carriage, that I am unable to paint.'

'And therefore . . . ?'

His Lordship seemed to be deriving an odd sort of pleasure from this as he urged Yoshihide to continue, but Yoshihide himself, red lips trembling as with a fever, could only repeat, as if in a dream, 'This is what I am unable to paint.'

Then suddenly, all but biting into his own words, he cried, 'I beg you, My Lord: have your men set a carriage on fire. Let me watch the flames devour its frame and its woven cabin. And, if possible –'

A dark cloud crossed His Lordship's face, but no sooner had it passed than he broke into a loud cackle. He was still choking with laughter when he spoke: '"Possible"? I'll do whatever you want. Don't waste time worrying about what is "possible."'

His Lordship's words filled me with a terrible foreboding. And in fact his appearance at that moment was anything but ordinary. White foam gathered at the corners of his mouth. His eyebrows convulsed into jagged bolts of lightning. It was as if His Lordship himself had become infused with Yoshihide's madness. And no sooner had he finished speaking than laughter – endless laughter – exploded from his throat once again.

'I'll burn a carriage for you,' he said. 'And I'll have a voluptuous woman inside it, dressed in a noblewoman's robes. She will die writhing with agony in flames and black smoke. – I have to salute you, Yoshihide. Who could have thought of such a thing but the greatest painter in the land?'

Yoshihide went pale when he heard this, and for a time the only part of him that moved was his lips: he seemed to be gasping for breath. Then, as though all the muscles of his body had gone limp at once, he crumpled forward with his hands on the matted floor again.

'A thousand thanks to you, My Lord,' Yoshihide said with rare humility, his voice barely audible. Perhaps the full horror of his own plan had come all too clear to him as he heard it spelled out in His Lordship's words. Only this one time in my life did I ever think of Yoshihide as a man to be pitied.

16

Two or three nights later, His Lordship summoned Yoshihide as promised to witness the burning of the carriage. He held the event not at the Horikawa mansion, but outside the Capital, at his late younger sister's mountain retreat, widely known as the 'Palace of the Melting Snows.'

No one had lived at this 'palace' for a very long time. Its spacious gardens had gone wild, and the desolate sight must have given rise to all sorts of rumors, many about His Lordship's sister, who had actually died there. People used to say that on moonless nights Her Ladyship's broad-skirted scarlet trousers would glide eerily along the outdoor corridor, never touching the floor. And no wonder there were such stories! The palace was lonely enough in the daytime, but once the sun set it became downright unnerving. The garden stream would murmur ominously in the darkness, and herons would swoop in the starlight like monstrous creatures.

As it happened, the carriage burning took place on one of those pitch-dark, moonless nights. Oil lamps revealed His Lordship seated in cross-legged ease on the veranda. Beneath a turquoise robe he wore deep-lavender patterned trousers. On a thick round mat edged in white brocade, his position was of course elevated above the half-dozen or so attendants who surrounded him. One among them appeared most eager to be of service to His Lordship, a burly samurai who had distinguished himself in the campaign against the northern barbarians some years earlier. He was said to have survived starvation by eating human flesh, after which he had the strength to tear out the antlers of a living stag with his bare hands. On this night he knelt in stern readiness below the veranda, in the scabbard at his armored waist a sword tipped up and back like a gull's tail, ready to be drawn at a moment's notice. These men presented a strangely terrifying, almost dreamlike spectacle. The lamplight flickering in the night wind turned them all dark one moment, bright the next.

And then there was the carriage itself. Even without an ox attached to its long black shafts, their ends resting on the usual low bench that tilted the whole slightly forward, it stood out against the night, its tall cabin woven of the finest split palm leaf, exactly as Yoshihide had requested: truly, a conveyance worthy of His Imperial Majesty or the most powerful ministers of state. When I saw its gold fittings gleaming like stars in the sky, and considered what was soon to happen to this lavishly appointed vehicle, a shiver went through me in spite of the warm spring night. As for what might be inside the carriage, there was no way to tell: its lovely blinds, woven of still-green bamboo and edged in patterned cloth, had been rolled down tight, and around it alert-looking conscripts stood guard, holding flaming torches and showing their concern that too much smoke might be drifting toward His Lordship on the veranda.

Yoshihide himself was situated at some remove, kneeling on the ground directly opposite the veranda. He wore what seemed to be his usual reddish-brown robe and tall black soft hat, and he looked especially small and shabby, as though the star-filled sky were a weight pressing down upon him. Behind him knelt another person in an outfit like his – probably an apprentice he had brought along. With them crouching down low in the darkness like that, I could not make out the color of their robes from my place below the veranda.

17

Midnight was approaching, I believe. I felt as if the darkness enveloping the garden were silently watching us all breathing, the only sound an occasional rush of night wind, each gust wafting toward us the resinous smell from the pine smoke of the torches. His Lordship remained silent for some moments, observing the mysterious scene, but then, edging forward where he sat, he cried sharply:

'Yoshihide!'

Yoshihide may have said some word in response, but to my ears it sounded like nothing so much as a moan.

'Tonight, Yoshihide, I am going to burn a carriage for you, as you requested.'

When he said this, His Lordship glanced at the men around him. I thought I saw a meaningful smile pass between him and certain of them. Of course, it could have been my imagination. Now Yoshihide seemed to be timidly raising his head and looking up toward the veranda, but still he waited, saying nothing.

'I want you to look at this,' His Lordship said. 'This is *my* carriage, the one I use every day. You know it well, I'm sure. I will now have it set afire in order that you may see the Hell of Searing Heat here on earth before your eyes.'

His Lordship reverted to silence and his eyes flashed another signal to his men. Then, with sudden vehemence, he cried, 'Chained inside the carriage is a sinful woman. When we set the carriage afire, her flesh will be roasted, her bones will be charred: she will die an agonizing death. Never again will you have such a perfect model for the screen. Do not fail to watch as her snow-white flesh erupts in flames. See and remember her long black hair dancing in a whirl of sparks!'

His Lordship sank into silence for yet a third time, but – whatever could have been in his mind? – now all he did was laugh soundlessly, his shoulders quaking.

'Never again will there be a sight like this, Yoshihide! I shall join you in observing it. All right, men, raise the blind. Let Yoshihide see the woman inside!'

On hearing this command, one of the conscripts, torch held high, strode up to the carriage, stretched out his free hand, and whipped the blind up. The torch crackled and flickered and cast its red gleam inside. On the carriage's matted floor, cruelly chained, sat a woman – and oh, who could have failed to recognize her? Her long black hair flowed in a voluptuous band across a gorgeous robe embroidered in cherry blossoms, and the golden hairpins on top of her downcast head sparkled beautifully in the firelight. For all the differences in costuming, there was no mistaking that girlish frame, that graceful neck (where now a gag was fastened), that touchingly modest profile: they belonged to none other than Yoshihide's daughter. I could hardly keep from crying out.

Just then the samurai kneeling across from me sprang to his feet and, pressing threateningly on his sword hilt, glared at Yoshihide. Startled by this sudden movement, I turned my gaze toward Yoshihide. He looked as if this spectacle were driving him half mad. Where he had been crouching until then, he was on his feet now and poised – arms outstretched – to run toward the carriage. Unfortunately, though, as I said before, he was in the shadows far away from me, and so I did not have a clear view of his face. My frustration lasted but a moment, however. Now, drained of color though it was, Yoshihide's face – or, should I say, Yoshihide's entire

45

form, raised aloft by some invisible power – appeared before me with such clarity it seemed to have cut its way through the surrounding darkness. For suddenly His Lordship had cried 'Burn it!', the conscripts flung their torches, and the carriage, with Yoshihide's daughter inside, burst into flame.

18

The fire engulfed the entire carriage. The purple roof tassels blew aside, then clouds of smoke swirled aloft, stark white against the blackness of the night, and finally a shower of sparks spurted upward with such terrifying force that in a single instant the blinds, the side panels, and the roof's metal fittings were ripped off in the blast and sent flying. Still more horrible was the color of the flames that licked the latticed cabin vents before shooting skyward, as though – might I say? – the sun itself had crashed to earth, spewing its heavenly fire in all directions. As close as I had come to crying out before, now I could only gape in mute awe at the horrifying spectacle.

But what of the girl's father?

I will never forget the look on Yoshihide's face at that moment. He had started toward the carriage on impulse but halted when the flames flared up. He then stood

there with arms outstretched, eyes devouring the smoke
and flames that enveloped the carriage. In the firelight
that bathed him from head to toe, I could see every fea-
ture of his ugly, wrinkled face. His wide-staring eyes, his
contorted lips, the twitching flesh of his cheeks: all drew
a vivid picture of the shock, the terror, and the sorrow
that traversed Yoshihide's heart by turns. Such anguish, I
suspect, would not be seen even on the face of a con-
victed thief about to have his head cut off or the guiltiest
sinner about to face the judgment of the Ten Kings of
Hell. Even the powerful samurai went pale at the sight
and stole a fearful glance at His Lordship above him.

But what of His Lordship himself? Biting his lip and
smiling strangely now and then, he stared straight
ahead, never taking his eyes off the carriage. And the girl
in the carriage – ah, I don't think I have the courage to
describe in detail what she looked like then. The pale
whiteness of her upturned face as she choked on the
smoke; the tangled length of her hair as she tried to shake
the flames from it; the beauty of her cherry-blossom
robe as it burst into flame: it was all so cruel, so terrible!
Especially at one point when the night wind rushed
down from the mountain to sweep away the smoke: the
sight of her against a flaming background of red flecked
with gold dust, gnawing at her gag, writhing as if to
snap the chains that bound her: it was enough to make

47

our flesh creep, not only mine but the powerful samurai's as well – as if the tortures of hell were being pictured right there before our eyes.

Just then the night wind gusted once more, rustling the branches of the garden's trees – or so it seemed to me and, I am sure, to everyone else. Such a sound seemed to race through the dark sky, and in that instant some black thing shot from the palace roof into the blazing carriage. It traveled in a perfectly straight line like a ball that has been kicked, neither touching the earth nor arcing through space. And as the carriage's burning side lattices collapsed inward, glowing as if coated in crimson lacquer, the thing grasped the girl's straining shoulders and hurled a long, piercing, and inexpressibly anguished scream out beyond the billowing smoke. Another scream followed, and then a third, until we all found ourselves crying out with it. For though it had been left tethered back at the Horikawa mansion, what we saw now clinging to the girl's shoulders against a flaming backdrop was the monkey Yoshihide.

19

We could see the monkey for only the briefest moment, though. A fountain of sparks shot up to the sky like gold dust in black lacquer, and then not only the monkey but the girl, too, was shrouded in black smoke. Now in the middle of the garden there was only a carriage of fire seething in flames with a terrible roar. No – 'pillar of fire' might better describe this horrific conflagration boiling up to the starry heavens.

But oh, how strange it was to see the painter now, standing absolutely rigid before the pillar of fire! Yoshihide – who only a few moments earlier had seemed to be suffering the torments of hell – stood there with his arms locked across his chest as if he had forgotten even the presence of His Lordship, his whole wrinkled face suffused now with an inexpressible radiance – the radiance of religious ecstasy. I could have sworn that the man's eyes were no longer watching his daughter dying in agony, that instead the gorgeous colors of flames and the sight of a woman suffering in them were giving him joy beyond measure.

The most wondrous thing was not that he watched his only daughter's death throes with apparent joy, but rather that Yoshihide at that moment possessed a strange, inhuman majesty that resembled the rage of the King of Beasts himself as you might see him in a dream. For this reason – although I might have been imagining it – the countless night birds that flew around us squawking in alarm at each new eruption of flames seemed to keep their distance from Yoshihide's tall black hat. Perhaps even these insentient birds could see the mysterious grandeur that hung above Yoshihide like a radiant aura.

If the birds could see it, how much more so the rest of us, down to the lowly conscripts. Trembling inwardly, scarcely breathing, and filled with a bizarre sense of adoration, we kept our eyes fastened on Yoshihide as if we were present at the decisive moment when a lump of stone or wood becomes a holy image of the Buddha. The carriage flames that filled the heavens with a roar; Yoshihide under the spell of the flames, transfixed: what sublimity! what rapture! But among us only one, His Lordship, looked on as if transformed into another person, his noble countenance drained of color, the corners of his mouth flecked with foam, hands clutching his knees through his lavender trousers as he panted like a beast in need of water . . .

20

Word soon spread that His Lordship had burned the carriage that night in the Palace of the Melting Snows, and there seem to have been many who were highly critical of the event. First of all came the question of

Yoshihide's daughter: why had His Lordship chosen to burn her alive? The rumor most often heard was that he had done it out of spite for her rejection of his love. I am certain, however, that he did it to punish the twisted personality of an artist who would go so far as to burn a carriage and kill a human being to complete the painting of a screen. In fact, I overheard His Lordship saying as much himself.

And then there was Yoshihide, whose stony heart was also apparently the topic of much negative commentary. How, after seeing his own daughter burned alive, could he want to finish the screen painting? Some cursed him as a beast in human guise who had forgotten a father's love for the sake of a picture. One who allied himself with this opinion was His Reverence the Abbot of Yokawa, who always used to say, 'Excel in his art though he might, if a man does not know the Five Virtues, he can only end up in hell.'

A month went by, and the screen with its images of hell was finished at last. Yoshihide brought it to the mansion that very day and humbly presented it for His Lordship's inspection. His Reverence happened to be visiting at the time, and I am certain that he was shocked at the sight of the horrible firestorm blasting through it. Until he actually saw the screen, he was glowering at Yoshihide, but then he slapped his knee and exclaimed, 'What magnificent work!' I can still see the bitter smile on His Lordship's face when he heard those words.

Almost no one spoke ill of Yoshihide after that – at least not in the mansion. Could it be because all who saw the screen – even those who had always hated him – were struck by strangely solemn feelings when they witnessed the tortures of the Hell of Searing Heat in all their reality?

By then, however, Yoshihide numbered among those who are no longer of this world. The night after he finished the screen, he tied a rope to a beam in his room and hanged himself. I suspect that, having sent his daughter on ahead to the other world, he could not bear to go on living here as if nothing had happened. His body lies buried in the ruins of his home. The little stone marker is probably so cloaked in moss now, after decades of exposure to the wind and rain, that no one can tell whose grave it is anymore.

The Spider Thread

I

And now, children, let me tell you a story about Lord Buddha Shakyamuni.

It begins one day as He was strolling alone in Paradise by the banks of the Lotus Pond. The blossoms on the pond were like perfect white pearls, and from their golden centers wafted forth a never-ending fragrance wonderful beyond description. I think it must have been morning in Paradise.

Soon Lord Shakyamuni stepped to the edge of the pond, where He glanced down through the spreading lotus leaves to the spectacle below. Directly beneath the Lotus Pond of Paradise lay the lower depths of Hell, and as He peered through the crystalline waters, He could see the River of Three Crossings and the Mountain of Needles as clearly as if He were viewing pictures in a peep-box.

Down there His eye came to rest upon a man named Kandata, who was writhing in Hell with all the other sinners. This great robber had done many evil deeds: he had even killed people, and burned down houses. But it seems that Kandata had performed one single act of goodness. Passing through a deep wood one day, he had noticed a tiny spider creeping along the wayside. His first thought was to stamp it to death, but as he raised his foot, he told himself, 'No, no. Even this puny creature is a living thing. To take its life for no reason would be too cruel.' And so he had let it pass unharmed.

Now, as He looked down at the nether world, Lord Shakyamuni recalled how Kandata had saved the spider, and He decided to reward him for it by delivering him from Hell if possible. By happy chance, He turned to see a heavenly spider spinning a beautiful silver thread atop a lotus leaf the color of shimmering jade. Gently lifting the spider thread, He lowered it straight down through the pearl-like blossoms to the depths far below.

2

Here, with the other sinners at the low-point of the lowest Hell, Kandata was endlessly floating up and sinking down again in the Pond of Blood. Wherever he looked there was only pitch darkness, and when a faint shape did pierce the shadows, it was the glint of a needle on the horrible Mountain of Needles, which only heightened his sense of doom. All was silent as the grave, and when a faint sound did break the stillness, it was the feeble sigh of a sinner. As you can imagine, those who had fallen this far had been so worn down by their tortures in the seven other hells that they no longer had the strength to cry out. Great robber though he was, Kandata could only thrash about like a dying frog as he choked on the blood of the pond.

And then, children, what do you think happened next? Yes, indeed: raising his head, Kandata chanced to look up toward the sky above the Pond of Blood and saw the gleaming silver spider thread, so slender and delicate, slipping stealthily down through the silent darkness from the high, high heavens, coming straight for *him*! Kandata clapped his hands in joy. If only he could take hold of this thread and climb up and up, he could probably escape from Hell. And maybe, with luck, he could even enter Paradise. Then he would never again be driven up the Mountain of Needles or plunged down into the Pond of Blood.

No sooner had the thought crossed his mind than Kandata grasped the spider thread and started climbing with all his might, higher and higher. As a great robber, Kandata had had plenty of practice at this kind of hand-over-hand rope climbing.

Hell and Heaven, though, are untold thousands of leagues apart, so it was not easy even for a man like Kandata to escape, no matter how hard he tried. He soon began to tire, until he couldn't raise his arm for even one more pull. He had no choice but to stop for a rest, and as he clung to the spider thread, he looked down far below.

Then he realized that all his climbing had been worth the effort: the Pond of Blood was hidden now in the depths of the darkness. And even the dull glint of the terrifying Mountain of Needles was far down beneath his feet. At this rate, it might be easier than he had imagined to climb his way out of Hell. Twining his hands in the spider thread, Kandata laughed aloud as he had not in all the years since he had come to this place: 'I've done it! I've done it!'

And then what do you think he saw? Far down on the spider thread, countless sinners had followed after him, and they were clambering up the thread with all their might like a column of ants! The sight struck him with such shock and fear that for a time his mouth gaped open like an idiot's; only his eyes moved. This slim thread seemed likely to snap from his weight alone:

how could it possibly hold so many people? If it were to break midway, then Kandata himself would plummet back down into the Hell he had struggled so mightily to escape. How terrible that would be! Still, from the pitch-dark Pond of Blood, an unbroken column of sinners came squirming up the fragile, gleaming thread by the hundreds – by the thousands. He knew he would have to do something now or the thread would break in two.

Kandata screamed at them, 'Listen to me, you sinners! This spider thread is *mine*! Who said *you* could climb it? Get off! Get off!'

At that very instant the spider thread, which until then had been perfectly fine, broke with a 'snap!' just where Kandata was hanging from it. Before he could even cry out, Kandata fell, slicing through the air, spinning like a top, down head-first into the darkest depths.

Behind him all that remained was the dangling short end of the spider thread from Paradise, delicately gleaming in the moonless, starless sky.

3

Standing at the edge of the Lotus Pond in Paradise, Lord Shakyamuni watched everything that happened.

Ryūnosuke Akutagawa

And when, in the end, Kandata sank like a stone into the Pond of Blood, the Holy One resumed His stroll, His face now tinged with sorrow. Kandata had thought to save himself alone, and as just punishment for this lack of compassion, he had fallen back into Hell. How shameful it must have seemed in the eyes of Lord Shakyamuni!

The lotuses of the Lotus Pond, however, were unperturbed. They swayed their perfect pearl-white blossoms near the feet of Lord Shakyamuni, and from their golden centers wafted forth each time a never-ending fragrance wonderful beyond description. I think it must have been close to noon in Paradise.

a little history

Penguin Modern Classics were launched in 1961, and have been shaping the reading habits of generations ever since.

The list began with distinctive grey spines and evocative pictorial covers – a look that, after various incarnations, continues to influence their current design – and with books that are still considered landmark classics today.

Penguin Modern Classics have caused scandal and political change, inspired great films and broken down barriers, whether social, sexual or the boundaries of language itself. They remain the most provocative, groundbreaking, exciting and revolutionary works of the last 100 years (or so).

In 2011, on the fiftieth anniversary of the Modern Classics, we're publishing fifty Mini Modern Classics: the very best short fiction by writers ranging from Beckett to Conrad, Nabokov to Saki, Updike to Wodehouse. Though they don't take long to read, they'll stay with you long after you turn the final page.

MODERN CLASSICS
www.penguinclassics.com